The St Spedague's Dropper

By

Sir Arthur Conan Doyle

Copyright © 2011 Read Books Ltd.
This book is copyright and may not be
reproduced or copied in any way without
the express permission of the publisher in writing

British Library Cataloguing-in-Publication Data
A catalogue record for this book is available from
the British Library

The Story of Spedegue's Dropper

by Sir Arthur Conan Doyle

The name of Walter Scougall needs no introduction to the cricketing public. In the 'nineties he played for his University. Early in the century he began that long career in the county team which carried him up to the War. That great tragedy broke his heart for games, but he still served on his county Club Committee and was reckoned one of the best judges of the game in the United Kingdom.

Scougall, after his abandonment of active sport, was wont to take his exercise by long walks through the New Forest, upon the borders of which he was living. Like all wise men, he walked very silently through that wonderful waste, and in that way he was often privileged to see sights which are lost to the average heavy-stepping wayfarer. Once, late in the evening, it was a badger blundering towards its hole under a hollow bank. Often a little group of deer would be glimpsed in the open rides. Occasionally a fox would steal across the path and then dart off at the sight of the noiseless wayfarer. Then one day he saw a human sight which was more strange than any in the animal world.

In a narrow glade there stood two great oaks. They were thirty or forty feet apart, and the glade was spanned by a cord which connected them up. This cord was at least fifty feet above the ground, and it must have entailed no small effort to get it there. At each side of the cord a cricket stump had been placed at the usual distance from each other. A tall, thin young man in spectacles was lobbing balls, of which he seemed to have a good supply, from one end, while at the other end a lad of sixteen, wearing wicket-keeper's gloves, was catching those which missed the wicket. "Catching" is the right word, for no ball struck the ground. Each was projected high up into the air and passed over the cord, descending at a very sharp angle on to the stumps.

Scougall stood for some minutes behind a holly bush watching this curious performance. At first it seemed pure lunacy, and then gradually he began to perceive a method in it. It was no easy matter to hurl a ball up over that cord and bring it down near the wicket. It needed a very correct trajectory. And yet this singular young man, using what the observer's practised eye recognized as a leg-break action which would entail a swerve in the air, lobbed up ball after ball either right on to the bails or into the wicket-keeper's hands just beyond them. Great practice was surely needed before he had attained such a degree of accuracy as this.

Finally his curiosity became so great that Scougall moved out into the glade, to the obvious surprise and embarrassment of the two performers. Had they been caught in some guilty action they could not have looked more unhappy. However, Scougall was a man of the world with a pleasant manner, and he soon put them at their ease.

"Excuse my butting in," said he. "I happened to be passing and I could not help being interested. I am an old cricketer, you see, and it appealed to me. Might I ask what you were trying to do?"

"Oh, I am just tossing up a few balls," said the elder, modestly. "You see, there is no decent ground about here, so my brother and I come out into the Forest."

"Are you a bowler, then?"

The Story of Spedegue's Dropper

"Well, of sorts."

"What club do you play for?"

"It is only Wednesday and Saturday cricket. Bishops Bramley is our village."

"But do you always bowl like that?"

"Oh, no. This is a new idea that I have been trying out."

"Well, you seem to get it pretty accurately."

"I am improving. I was all over the place at first. I didn't know what parish they would drop in. But now they are usually there or about it."

"So I observe."

"You said you were an old cricketer. May I ask your name?"

"Walter Scougall."

The young man looked at him as a young pupil looks at the world-famed master.

"You remember the name, I see."

"Walter Scougall. Oxford and Hampshire. Last played in 1913. Batting average for that season, twenty-seven point five. Bowling average, sixteen for seventy-two wickets."

"Good Lord!"

The younger man, who had come across, burst out laughing.

"Tom is like that," said he. "He is Wisden and Lillywhite rolled into one. He could tell you anyone's record, and every county's record for this century."

"Well, well! What a memory you must have!"

"Well, my heart is in the game," said the young man, becoming amazingly confidential, as shy men will when they find a really sympathetic listener. "But it's my heart that won't let me play it as I should wish to do. You see, I get asthma if I do too much—and palpitations. But they play me at Bishops Bramley for my slow bowling, and so long as I field slip I don't have too much running to do."

"You say you have not tried these lobs, or whatever you may call them, in a match?"

"No, not yet. I want to get them perfect first. You see, it was my ambition to invent an entirely new ball. I am sure it can be done. Look at Bosanquet and the googlie. Just by using his brain he thought of and worked out the idea of concealed screw on the ball. I said to myself that Nature had handicapped me with a weak heart, but not with a weak brain, and that I might think out some new thing which was within the compass of my strength. Droppers, I call them. Spedegue's droppers—that's the name they may have some day."

Scougall laughed. "I don't want to discourage you, but I wouldn't bank on it too much," said he. "A quick-eyed batsman would simply treat them as he would any other full toss and every ball would be a boundary."

Spedegue's face fell. The words of Scougall were to him as the verdict of the High Court judge. Never had he spoken before with a first-class cricketer, and he had hardly the nerve to defend his own theory. It was the younger one who spoke.

"Perhaps, Mr. Scougall, you have hardly thought it all out yet," said he. "Tom has given it a lot of consideration. You see, if the ball is tossed high enough it has a great pace as it falls. It's really like having a fast bowler from above. That's his idea. Then, of course, there's the field."

"Ah, how would you place your field?"

"All on the on side bar one or two at the most," cried Tom Spedegue, taking up the argument. "I've nine to dispose of. I should have mid-off well up. That's all. Then I should have eight men to leg, three on the boundary, one mid-on, two square, one fine, and one a rover, so that the batsman would never quite know where he was. That's the idea."

Scougall began to be serious. It was clear that this young fellow really had plotted the thing out. He walked across to the wicket.

"Chuck up one or two," said he. "Let me see how they look." He brandished his walking-stick and waited expectant. The ball soared in the air and came down with unexpected speed just over the stump. Scougal looked more serious still. He had seen many cricket balls, but never quite from that angle, and it gave him food for thought.

"Have you ever tried it in public?"

"Never."

"Don't you think it is about time?"

"Yes, I think I might."

"When?"

"Well, I'm not generally on as a first bowler. I am second change as a rule. But if the skipper will let me have a go——"

"I'll see to that," said Scougall. "Do you play at Bishops Bramley?"

"Yes; it is our match of the year—against Mudford, you know."

"Well, I think on Saturday I'd like to be there and see how it works."

Sure enough Scougall turned up at the village match, to the great

The Story of Spedegue's Dropper

excitement of the two rural teams. He had a serious talk with the home captain, with the result that for the first time in his life Tom Spedegue was first bowler for his native village. What the other village thought of his remarkable droppers need not influence us much, since they would probably have been got out pretty cheaply by any sort of bowling. None the less, Scougall watched the procession to and from the cow-shed which served as a pavilion with an appreciative eye, and his views as to the possibilities lying in the dropper became clearer than before. At the end of the innings he touched the bowler upon the shoulder.

"That seems all right," he said.

"No, I couldn't quite get the length—and, of course, they did drop catches."

"Yes, I agree that you could do better. Now look here! you are second master at a school, are you not?"

"That is right."

"You could get a day's leave if I wangled with the chief?"

"It might be done."

"Well, I want you next Tuesday. Sir George Sanderson's house-party team is playing the Free Foresters at Ringwood. You must bowl for Sir George."

Tom Spedegue flushed with pleasure.

"Oh, I say!" was all he could stammer out.

"I'll work it somehow or other. I suppose you don't bat?"

"Average nine," said Spedegue, proudly.

Scougall laughed. "Well, I noticed that you were not a bad fielder near the wicket."

"I usually hold them."

"Well, I'll see your boss, and you will hear from me again."

Scougall was really taking a great deal of trouble in this small affair, for he went down to Totton and saw the rather grim head master. It chanced, however, that the old man had been a bit of a sport in his day, and he relaxed when Scougall explained the inner meaning of it all. He laughed incredulously, however, and shook his head when Scougall whispered some aspiration.

"Nonsense!" was his comment.

"Well, there is a chance."

"Nonsense!" said the old man once again.

"It would be the making of your school."

"It certainly would," the headmaster replied. "But it is nonsense all the same."

Scougall saw the head master again on the morning after the Free Foresters match.

"You see it works all right," he said.

"Yes, against third-class men."

"Oh, I don't know. Donaldson was playing, and Murphy. They were not so bad. I tell you they are the most amazed set of men in Hampshire. I have bound them all over to silence."

"Why?"

"Surprise is the essence of the matter. Now I'll take it a stage farther. By Jove, what a joke it would be!" The old cricketer and the sporting schoolmaster roared with laughter as they thought of the chances of the future.

All England was absorbed in one question at that moment. Politics, business, even taxation had passed from people's minds. The one engrossing subject was the fifth Test Match. Twice England had won by a narrow margin, and twice Australia had barely struggled to victory. Now in a week Lord's was to be the scene of the final and crucial battle of giants. What were the chances, and how was the English team to be made up?

It was an anxious time for the Selection Committee, and three more harassed men than Sir James Gilpin, Mr. Tarding and Dr. Sloper were not to be found in London. They sat now in the committee-room of the great pavilion, and they moodily scanned the long list of possibles which lay before them, weighing the claims of this man or that, closely inspecting the latest returns from the county matches, and arguing how far a good all-rounder was a better bargain than a man who was supremely good in one department but weak in another—such men, for example, as Worsley of Lancashire, whose average was seventy-one, but who was a sluggard in the field, or Scott of Leicestershire, who was near the top of the bowling and quite at the foot of the batting averages. A week of such work had turned the committee into three jaded old men.

"There is the question of endurance," said Sir James, the man of many years and much experience. 'A three days' match is bad enough, but this is to be played out and may last a week. Some of these top average men are getting on in years."

The Story of Spedegue's Dropper

"Exactly," said Tarding, who had himself captained England again and again. "I am all for young blood and new methods. The trouble is that we know their bowling pretty well, and as for them on a marled wicket they can play ours with their eyes shut. Each side is likely to make five hundred per innings, and a very little will make the difference between us and them."

"It's just that very little that we have got to find," said solemn old Dr. Sloper, who had the reputation of being the greatest living authority upon the game. "If we could give them something new! But, of course, they have played every county and sampled everything we have got."

"What can we ever have that is new?" cried Tarding. "It is all played out."

"Well, I don't know," said Sir James. "Both the swerve and the googlie have come along in our time. But Bosanquets don't appear every day. We want brain as well as muscle behind the ball."

"Funny we should talk like this," said Dr. Sloper, taking a letter from his pocket. "This is from old Scougall, down in Hampshire. He says he is at the end of a wire and is ready to come up if we want him. His whole argument is on the very lines we have been discussing. New blood, and a complete surprise—that is his slogan."

"Does he suggest where we are to find it?"

"Well, as a matter of fact he does. He has dug up some unknown fellow from the back of beyond who plays for the second eleven of the Mudtown Blackbeetles or the Hinton Chawbacons or some such team, and he wants to put him straight in to play for England. Poor old Scougie has been out in the sun."

"At the same time there is no better captain than Scougall used to be. I don't think we should put his opinion aside too easily. What does he say?"

"Well, he is simply red-hot about it. 'A revelation to me.' That is one phrase. 'Could not have believed it if I had not seen it.' 'May find it out afterwards, but it is bound to upset them the first time.' That is his view."

"And where is this wonder man?"

"He has sent him up so that we can see him if we wish. Telephone the Thackeray Hotel, Blooomsbury."

"Well, what do you say?"

"Oh, it's pure waste of time," said Tarding. "Such things don't happen, you know. Even if we approved of him, what would the country think and what would the Press say?"

Sir James stuck out his grizzled jaw.

"Damn the country and the Press, too!" said he. "We are here to follow our own judgment, and I jolly well mean to do so."

"Exactly," said Dr. Sloper.

Tarding shrugged his broad shoulders.

"We have enough to do without turning down a side-street like that," said he. "However, if you both think so, I won't stand in the way. Have him up by all means and let us see what we make of him."

Half an hour later a very embarrassed young man was standing in front of the famous trio and listening to a series of very searching questions, to which he was giving such replies as he was able. Much of the ground which Scougall had covered in the Forest was explored by them once more.

"It boils down to this, Mr. Spedegue. You've once in your life played in good company. That is the only criterion. What exactly did you do?"

Spedegue pulled a slip of paper, which was already frayed from much use, out of his waistcoat pocket.

"This is *The Hampshire Telegraph* account, sir."

Sir James ran his eye over it and read snatches aloud. "Much amusement was caused by the bowling of Mr. T. E. Spedegue." "Hum! That's rather two-edged. Bowling should not be a comic turn. After all, cricket is a serious game. Seven wickets for thirty-four. Well, that's better. Donaldson is a good man. You got him, I see. And Murphy, too! Well, now, would you mind going into the pavilion and waiting? You will find some pictures there that will amuse you if you value the history of the game. We'll send for you presently."

When the youth had gone the Selection Committee looked at each other in puzzled silence.

"You simply can't do it!" said Tarding at last. "You can't face it. To play a bumpkin like that because he once got seven wickets for thirty-four in country-house cricket is sheer madness. I won't be a party to it."

"Wait a bit, though! Wait a bit!" cried Sir James. "Let us thresh it out a little before we decide."

So they threshed it out, and in half an hour they sent for Tom Spedegue once more. Sir James sat with his elbows on the table and his finger-tips touching while he held forth in his best judicial maner. His conclusion was a remarkable one.

"So it comes to this, Mr. Spedegue, that we all three want to be on surer ground before we take a step which would rightly expose us to the most tremendous public criticism. You will therefore remain in London, and at three-forty-five to-morrow morning, which is just after dawn, you will come down in your flannels to the side entrance of Lord's. We will, under pledge of secrecy, assemble twelve or thirteen groundmen whom we can trust, including half-a-dozen first-class bats. We will have a wicket prepared on the practice ground, and we will try you out under proper conditions with your ten fielders and all. If you fail, there is an end. If you make good, we may consider your claim."

"Good gracious, sir, I made no claim."

"Well, your friend Scougall did for you. But anyhow, that's how we have fixed it. We shall be there, of course, and a few others whose opinion we can trust. If you care to wire Scougall he can come too. But the whole thing is secret, for we quite see the point that it must be a complete surprise or a wash-out. So you will keep your mouth shut and we shall do the same."

Thus it came about that one of the most curious games in the history of cricket was played on the Lord's ground next morning. There is a high wall round that part, but early wayfarers as they passed were amazed to hear the voices of the players, and the occasional crack of the ball at such an hour. The superstitious might almost have imagined that the spirits of the great departed were once again at work, and that the adventurous explorer might get a peep at the bushy black beard of the old giant or Billie Murdoch leading his Cornstalks once more to victory. At six o'clock the impromptu match was over, and the Selection Committee had taken the bravest and most sensational decision that had ever been hazarded since first a team was chosen. Tom Spedegue should play next week for England.

"Mind you," said Tarding, "if the beggar lets us down I simply won't face the music. I warn you of that. I'll have a taxi waiting at the gate and a passport in my pocket. Poste restante, Paris. That's me for the rest of the summer."

"Cheer up, old chap," said Sir James. "Our conscience is clear. We have acted for the best. Dash it all, we have ten good men, anyhow. If the worst came to the worst, it only means one passenger in the team."

"But it won't come to the worst," said Dr. Sloper, stoutly. "Hang it, we have seen with our own eyes. What more can we do? All the same, for the first time in my life I'll have a whisky-and-soda before breakfast."

Next day the list was published and the buzz began. Ten of the men might have been expected. These were Challen and Jones, as fast bowlers, and Widley, the slow left-hander. Then Peters, Moir, Jackson, Wilson, and Grieve were at the head of the batting averages, none of them under fifty, which was pretty good near the close of a wet season. Hanwell and Gordon were two all-rounders who were always sure of their places, dangerous bats, good change bowlers, and as active as cats in the field. So far so good. But who the Evil One was Thomas E. Spedegue? Never was there such a ferment in Fleet Street and such blank ignorance upon the part of "our well-informed correspondent." Special Commissioners darted here and there, questioning well-known cricketers, only to find that they were as much in the dark as themselves. Nobody knew—or if anyone did know, he was bound by oath not to tell. The wildest tales flew abroad. "We are able to assure the public that Spedegue is a 'nom de jeu' and conceals the identity of a world-famed cricketer who for family reasons is not permitted to reveal his true self." "Thomas E. Spedegue will surprise the crowd at Lord's by appearing as a coal-black gentleman from Jamaica. He came over with the last West Indian team, settled in Derbyshire, and is now eligible to play for England, though why he should be asked to do so is still a mystery." "Spedegue, as is now generally known, is a half-caste Malay who exhibited extraordinary cricket proficiency some years ago in Rangoon. It is said that he plays in a loincloth and can catch as well with his feet as with his hands. The question of whether he is qualified for England is a most debatable one." "Spedegue, Thomas E., is the headmaster of a famous northern school whose wonderful talents in the cricket field have been concealed by his devotion to his academic duties. Those who know him best are assured," etc., etc. The Committee also began to get it in the neck. "Why, with the wealth of talent available, these three elderly gentlemen, whose ideas of selection seem to be to pick names out of a bag, should choose one who, whatever his hidden virtues, is certainly unused to first-class cricket, far less to Test Matches, is one of those things which make one realize that the lunacy laws are not sufficiently comprehensive." These were fair samples of the comments.

The Story of Spedegue's Dropper

And then the inevitable came to pass. When Fleet Street is out for something it invariably gets it. No one quite knows how *The Daily Sportsman* succeeded in getting at Thomas Spedegue, but it was a great scoop and the incredible secret was revealed. There was a leader and there was an interview with the village patriarch which set London roaring with laughter. "No, we ain't surprised nohow," said Gaffer Hobbs. "Maister Spedegue do be turble clever with them slow balls of his'n. He sure was too much for them chaps what came in the char-à-bancs from Mudford. Artful, I call 'im. You'll see." The leader was scathing. "The Committee certainly seem to have taken leave of their senses. Perhaps there is time even now to alter their absurd decision. It is almost an insult to our Australian visitors. It is obvious that the true place for Mr. Thomas Spedegue, however artful he may be, is the village green and not Lord's, and that his competence to deal with the char-à-bancers of Mudford is a small guarantee that he can play first-class cricket. The whole thing is a deplorable mistake, and it is time that pressure was put upon the Selection Board to make them reconsider their decision."

"We have examined the score-book of the Bishops Bramley village club," wrote another critic. "It is kept in the tap-room of The Spotted Cow, and makes amusing reading. Our Test Match aspirant is hard to trace, as he played usually for the second eleven, and in any case there was no one capable of keeping an analysis. However, we must take such comfort as we can from his batting averages. This year he has actually amassed a hundred runs in nine recorded innings. Best in an innings, fifteen. Average, eleven. Last year he was less fortunate and came out with an average of nine. The youth is second master at the Totton High School and is in indifferent health, suffering from occasional attacks of asthma. And he is chosen to play for England! Is it a joke or what? We think that the public will hardly see the humour of it, nor will the Selection Committee find it a laughing matter if they persist in their preposterous action." So spoke the Press, but there were, it is only fair to say, other journals which took a more charitable view. "After all," said the sporting correspondent of *The Times*, "Sir James and his two colleagues are old and experienced players with a unique knowledge of the game. Since we have placed our affairs in their hands we must be content to leave them there. They have their own knowledge and their own private information of which we are ignorant. We can but trust them and await the event."

As to the three, they refused in any way to compromise or to bend to the storm. They gave no explanations, made no excuses, and simply dug in and lay quiet. So the world waited till the day came round.

We all remember what glorious weather it was. The heat and the perfect Bulli-earth wicket, so far as England could supply that commodity, reminded our visitors of their native conditions. It was England, however, who got the best of that ironed shirt-front wicket, for in their first knock even Cotsmore, the Australian giant, who was said to be faster than Gregory and more wily than Spofforth, could seldom get the ball bail-high. He bowled with splendid vim and courage, but his analysis at the end of the day only showed three wickets for a hundred and forty-two. Storr, the googlie merchant had a better showing with four for ninety-six. Cade's mediums accounted for two wickets, and Moir, the English captain, was run out. He had made seventy-three first, and Peters, Grieve, and Hanwell raked up sixty-four, fifty-seven, and fifty-one respectively, while nearly everyone was in double figures. The only exception was "Thomas E. Spedegue, Esq.," to quote the score card, which recorded a blank after his name. He was caught in the slips off the fast bowler, and, as he admitted afterwards that he had never for an instant seen the ball, and could hardly in his nervousness see the bowler, it is remarkable that his wicket was intact. The English total was four hundred and thirty-two, and the making of it consumed the whole of the first day. It was fast scoring in the time, and the crowd were fully satisfied with the result.

And now came the turn of Australia. An hour before play began forty thousand people had assembled, and by the time that the umpires came out the gates had to be closed, for there was not standing room within those classic precincts. Then came the English team, strolling out to the wickets and tossing the ball from hand to hand in time-honoured fashion. Finally appeared the two batsmen, Morland, the famous Victorian, the man of the quick feet and the supple wrists, whom many looked upon as the premier batsman of the world, and the stonewaller, Donahue, who had broken the hearts of so many bowlers with his obdurate defence. It was he who took the first over, which was delivered by Challen of Yorkshire, the raging, tearing fast bowler of the North. He sent down six beauties, but each of them came back to him down the pitch from that impenetrable half-cock shot which was characteristic of the famous Queenslander. It was a maiden over.

The Story of Spedegue's Dropper

And now Moir tossed the ball to Spedegue and motioned him to begin at the pavilion end. The English captain had been present at the surreptitious trial and he had an idea of the general programme, but it took him some time and some consultation with the nervous, twitching bowler before he could set the field. When it was finally arranged the huge audience gasped with surprise and the batsmen gazed round them as if they could hardly believe their eyes. One poor little figure, alone upon a prairie, broke the solitude of the off-side. He stood as a deep point or as a silly mid-off. The on-side looked like a mass meeting. The fielders were in each other's way, and kept shuffling about to open up separate lines. It too some time to arrange, while Spedegue stood at the crease with a nervous smile, fingering the ball and waiting for orders. The Selection Board were grouped in the open window of the committee-room, and their faces were drawn and haggard.

"My God! This is awful!" muttered Tarding.

"Got that cab?" asked Dr. Sloper, with a ghastly smile.

"Got it! It is my one stand-by."

"Room for three in it?" said Sir James. "Gracious, he has got five short-legs and no slip. Well, well, get to it! Anything is better than waiting."

There was a deadly hush as Spedegue delivered his first ball. It was an ordinary slow full pitch straight on the wicket. At any other time Morland would have slammed it to the boundary, but he was puzzled and cautious after all this mysterious setting of the field. Some unknown trap seemed to have been set for him. Therefore he played the ball quietly back to the bowler and set himself for the next one, which was similar and treated the same way.

Spedegue had lost his nerve. He simply could not, before this vast multitude of critics, send up the grotesque ball which he had invented. Therefore he compromised, which was the most fatal of all courses. He lobbed up balls which were high but not high enough. They were simply ordinary overpitched, full-toss deliveries such as a batsman sees when he has happy dreams and smiles in his sleep. Such was the third ball, which was a little to the off. Morland sent it like a bullet past the head of the lonely mid-off and it crashed against the distant rails. The three men in the window looked at each other and the sweat was on their brows. The next ball was again a juicy full toss on the level of the batsman's ribs. He banged it through the crowd of fielders on the on with a deft turn of the wrist which insured that it should be upon the ground. Then, gaining confidence, he waited for the next of those wonderful dream balls, and steadying himself for a mighty fast-footed swipe he knocked it clean over the ring and on to the roof of the hotel to square-leg. There were roars of applause, for a British crowd loves a lofty hit, whoever may deliver it. The scoreboard marked fourteen made off five balls. Such an opening to a Test Match had never be seen.

"We thought he might break a record, and by Jove he has!" said Tarding, bitterly. Sir James chewed his ragged moustache and Sloper twisted his fingers together in agony. Moir, who was fielding at mid-on, stepped across to the unhappy bowler.

"Chuck 'em up, as you did on Tuesday morning. Buck up, man! Don't funk it! You'll do them yet."

Spedegue grasped the ball convulsively and nerved himself to send it high into the air. For a moment he picture the New Forest glade, the white line of cord, and his young brother waiting behind the stump. But his nerve was gone, and with it his accuracy. There were roars of laughter as the ball went fifty feet into the air, which were redoubled when the wicket-keeper had to sprint back in order to catch it and the umpire stretched his arms out to signal a wide.

For the last ball, as he realized, that he was likely to bowl in the match, Spedegue approached the crease. The field was swimming round him. That yell of laughter which had greeted his effort had been the last straw. His nerve was broken. But there is a point when pure despair and desperation come to a man's aid—when he says to himself, "Nothing matters now. All is lost. It can't be worse than it is. Therefore I may as well let myself go." Never in all his practice had he bowled a ball as high as the one which now, to the amused delight of the crowd, went soaring into the air. Up it went and up—the most absurd ball ever delivered in a cricket match. The umpire broke down and shrieked with laughter, while even the amazed fielders joined in the general yell. The ball, after its huge parabola, descended well over the wicket, but as it was still within reach Morland, with a broad grin on his sunburned face, turned round and tapped it past the wicket-keeper's ear to the boundary. Spedegue's face drooped towards the ground. The bitterness of death was on him. It was all over. He had let down the Committee, he had let down the side, he had let down England. He wished the ground would open and swallow him so that his only memorial should be a scar upon the pitch of Lord's.

The Story of Spedegue's Dropper

And then suddenly the derisive laughter of the crowd was stilled, for it was seen that an incredible thing had happened. Morland was walking towards the pavilion. As he passed Spedegue he made a good-humoured flourish of his bat as if he would hit him over the head with it. At the same time the wicket-keeper stooped and picked something off the ground. It was a bail. Forgetful of his position and with all his thoughts upon this extraordinary ball which was soaring over his head, the great batsman had touched the wicket with his toe. Spedegue had a respite. The laughter was changing to applause. Moir came over and clapped him jovially upon the back. The scoring board showed total fifteen, last man fourteen, wickets one.

Challen sent down another over of fizzers to the impenetrable Donahue which resulted in a snick for two and a boundary off his legs. And then off the last ball a miracle occurred. Spedegue was field at fine slip, when he saw a red flash come towards him low on the right. He thrust out a clutching hand and there was the beautiful new ball right in the middle of his tingling palm. How it got there he had no idea, but what odds so long as the stonewaller would stonewall no more? Spedegue, from being the butt, was becoming the hero of the crowd. They cheered rapturously when he approached the crease for his second over. The board was twenty-one, six, two.

But now it was a different Spedegue. His fears had fallen from him. His confidence had returned. If he did nothing more he had at least done his share. But he would do much more. It had all come back to him, his sense of distance, his delicacy of delivery, his appreciation of curves. He had found his length and he meant to keep it.

The splendid Australian batsmen, those active, clear-eyed men who could smile at our fast bowling and make the best of our slow bowlers seem simple, were absolutely at sea. Here was something of which they had never heard, for which they had never prepared, and which was unlike anything in the history of cricket. Spedegue had got his fifty-foot trajectory to a nicety, bowling over the wicket with a marked curve from the leg. Every ball fell on or near the top of the stumps. He was as accurate as a human howitzer pitching shells. Batten, who followed Morland, hit across one of them and was clean bowled. Staker tried to cut one off his wicket, and knocked down his own off-stump, broke his bat, and finally saw the ball descend amid the general *débris*. Here and there one was turned to leg and once a short one was hit out of the ground. The fast bowler sent the fifth batsman's leg-stump flying and the score was five for thirty-seven. Then in successive balls Spedegue got Bollard and Whitelaw, the one caught at the wicket and the other at short square-leg. There was a stand between Moon and Carter, who put on twenty runs between them with a succession of narrow escapes from the droppers. Then each of them became victims, one getting his body in front, and the other being splendidly caught by Hanwell on the ropes. The last man was run out and the innings closed for seventy-four.

The crowd had begun by cheering and laughing, but now they had got beyond it and sat in a sort of awed silence as people might who were contemplating a miracle. Half-way through the innings Tarding had leaned forward and had grasped the hand of each of his colleagues. Sir James leaned back in his deck-chair and lit a large cigar. Dr. Sloper mopped his brow with his famous red handkerchief. "It's all right, but, by George! I wouldn't go through it again," he murmured. The effect upon the players themselves was curious. The English seemed apologetic, as though not sure themselves that such novel means could be justified. The Australians were dazed and a little resentful. "What price quoits?" said Batten, the captain, as he passed into the pavilion. Spedegue's figures were seven wickets for thirty-one.

And now the question arose whether the miracle would be repeated. Once more Donahue and Morland were at the wicket. As to the poor stonewaller, it was speedily apparent that he was helpless. How can you stonewall a ball which drops perpendicularly upon your bails? He held his bat flat before it as it fell in order to guard his wicket, and it simply popped up three feet into the air and was held by the wicket-keeper. One for nothing. Batten and Staker both hit lustily to leg and each was caught by the mass meeting who waited for them. Soon, however, it became apparent that the new attack was not invincible, and that a quick, adaptive batsman could find his own methods. Morland again and again brought off what is now called the back drive—a stroke unheard of before—when he turned and tapped the ball over the wicket-keeper's head to the boundary. Now that a crash helmet has been added to the stumper's equipment he is safer than he used to be, but Grieve has admitted that he was glad that he had a weekly paper with an insurance coupon in his cricket bag that day. A fielder was placed on the boundary in line with the stumps, and then the versatile Morland proceeded to elaborate those fine tips to slip and tips to fine leg which are admitted now to be the only proper treatment of the dropper. At the same time Whitelaw took a pace back so as to be level with his wicket and topped the droppers down to the off so that Spedegue had to bring two of his legs across and so disarrange his whole plan of campaign. The pair put on ninety for the fifth wicket, and when Whitelaw at last got out, bowled by Hanwell, the score stood at one hundred and thirty.

But from then onwards the case was hopeless. It is all very well for a quick-eyed active genius like Morland to adapt himself in a moment to a new game, but it is too much to ask of the average first-class cricketer, who, of all men, is most accustomed to routine methods. The slogging bumpkin from the village green would have made a better job of Spedegue than did these great cricketers, to whom the orthodox method was the only way. Every rule learned, every experience endured, had in a moment become useless. How could you play with a straight bat at a ball that fell from the clouds? They did their best—as well, probably, as the English team would have done in their place—but their best made a poor show upon a scoring card. Morland remained a great master to the end and carried out his bat for a superb seventy-seven. The second innings came to a close at six o'clock on the second day of the match, the score being one hundred and seventy-four. Spedegue eight for sixty-one. England had won by an innings and one hundred and eighty-four runs.

Well, it was a wonderful day and it came to a wonderful close. It is a matter of history how the crowd broke the ropes, how they flooded the field, and how Spedegue, protesting loudly, was carried shoulder-high into the pavilion. Then came the cheering and the speeches. The hero of the day had to appear again and again. When they were weary of cheering him they cheered for Bishops Bramley. Then the English captain had to make a speech. "Rather stand up to Cotsmore bowling on a ploughed field," said he. Then it was the turn of Batten the Australian. "You've beat us at something," he said ruefully; "don't quite know yet what it is. It's not what we call cricket down under." Then the Selection Board were called for and they had the heartiest and best deserved cheer of them all. Tarding told them about the waiting cab. "It's waiting yet," he said, "but I think I can now dismiss it."

Spedegue played no more cricket. His heart would not stand it. His doctor declared that this one match had been one too many and that he must stand out in the future. But for good or for bad—for bad, as many think—he has left his mark upon the game for ever. The English were more amused than exultant over their surprise victory. The Australian papers were at first inclined to be resentful, but then the absurdity that a man from the second eleven of an unknown club should win a Test Match began to soak into them, and finally Sydney and Melbourne had joined London in its appreciation of the greatest joke in the history of cricket.